First Experiences

THE
NEW PUPPY

Anne Civardi
Illustrated by Stephen Cartwright

Language Consultant: Betty Root
Reading and Language Information Centre
University of Reading, England

There is a little yellow duck hiding on every page. Can you find it?

The Applebys

This is the Appleby family. Ollie and Amber are very excited. They are going to fetch their new puppy.

Hazel Hill's House

Dad drives them to Hazel Hill's house. Eight weeks ago, her dog, Tina, had six tiny puppies.

Tina's Puppies

The puppies are playing in Hazel's house.
"Which one shall we choose, Mum?" says Ollie.

Choosing a Puppy

The smallest puppy runs up to the children. "I like this one best," says Ollie. "Me too," agrees Amber.

Taking Shrimp Home

Ollie carries the puppy to the car. "She's so little," says Amber, " let's call her Shrimp."

Shrimp meets Brat

When they get home, Ollie shows Shrimp her new bed. But Shrimp is more interested in Brat, the cat.

Feeding Shrimp

"I think Shrimp's hungry," says Ollie to Amber. "Let's give her some food."

Ollie and Amber give Shrimp a bowl of milk and some meat. But Shrimp is much too excited to eat.

In the Garden

They take her outside into the garden. "Perhaps Shrimp wants to do a wee?" says Amber.

At the Vet

Later, Dad, Ollie and Amber take Shrimp to the vet.
Shrimp wants to play with the other animals.

Shrimp has an Injection

The vet gives Shrimp an injection so that she will not get ill. "This won't hurt her," says the vet.

Goodnight Shrimp

After supper, Ollie puts Shrimp to bed. "Please can I
sleep with her, Mum?" asks Amber. "No," says Mum.

Time for Bed

Dad carries Amber upstairs. "Come on, sleepyhead,"
he says. "Goodnight, sleep tight, Shrimp," says Ollie.

What a Mess

The next morning, Ollie and Amber run to see
Shrimp. "Oh, what a mess," cries Amber.

Training Shrimp

There is a big puddle on the floor. Mum shows it to Shrimp. "Naughty girl", she says, softly.

On the Lead

Then Amber and Ollie take Shrimp for a walk. "I love our new puppy," says Amber. "Me too," agrees Ollie.

First published in 1988. Usborne Publishing Ltd, 20 Garrick Street, London WC2E 9BJ, England. © Usborne Publishing Ltd, 1988.